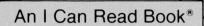

An I Can Read Book®

MR. SNIFF
AND THE MOTEL MYSTERY

Thomas P. Lewis

PICTURES BY
BETH LEE WEINER

HarperCollins*Publishers*

This book is a presentation of Atlas Editions Inc.
For further information about Atlas Editions book clubs for children
write to: **Atlas Editions, Inc.,**
    4343 Equity Drive,
    Columbus, Ohio 43228

Published by arrangement with HarperCollins Publishers.
I Can Read Book is a registered trademark of HarperCollins Publishers.

1998 Edition

Library of Congress Cataloging in Publication Data
Lewis, Thomas P.
   Mr. Sniff and the motel mystery.

   (An I can read book)
   Summary: The famous detective hound discovers why guests
are being frightened away from a beach motel.
   [1. Dogs—Fiction. 2. Mystery and detective stories]
I. Woldin, Beth Weiner, 1955—ill. II. Title. III. Title: Mister Sniff
and the motel mystery.
PZ7.L5882Mr 1984   [E]   82-47729
ISBN 0-06-023824-0
ISBN 0-06-02382.5-9 (lib. bdg.)

Printed in the U. S. A

Mr. Sniff was reading a newspaper
by the motel pool.
Suddenly he heard someone cry,
"Help! Help!"
Mr. Sniff was on his feet.

"Come quickly!"

called the guest in Room 17.

Mr. Sniff followed her inside.

Someone had written

"Help! Help!"

all over the bathroom mirror.

"Hm, lipstick," he said.

Mr. Sniff tasted the letters.

"I wonder what kind it is.

And this little fellow,"

said Mr. Sniff,

"should be in the mud,

or by some rocks—

not on your shirt!"

He picked a small spider crab

off the lady's shoulder.

"Someone wants to frighten me,"

said the guest.

Just then Mr. Mutt,

the owner of the motel, rushed in.

"What is the trouble,

Madame Bassett?" he asked.

Suddenly,

they heard shouts outside.

"Now what?" said Mr. Mutt.

"Let us see," said Mr. Sniff.

Many guests were standing
around the motel pool.
A ten-inch jellyfish
was swimming back and forth
in the water.

"Ugh! Will you look at that!"

said a man with big glasses.

"You won't catch *me* in there,"

another guest said.

12

Mr. Sniff reached over

and picked up the jellyfish.

"Hmm. Bluish white.

A moon jelly.

Harmless, but messy."

13

"This is too much," said Mr. Mutt.

"Who could have put it in the pool?

All my guests will leave.

I will lose my business.

Mr. Sniff, please help me!"

"You are my friend, Herman,"

said Mr. Sniff.

"I will begin at once."

"Can I help?" asked Andy Mutt.

"I know where everything is."

Andy was Mr. Mutt's youngest son.

"Very well," said Mr. Sniff.

"I will need keys to all the rooms."

"Jill has all the keys," said Andy.

"She is the summer maid."

"Let us go and see her,"

said Mr. Sniff.

They found Jill by the soda machine.

"Hi," said Andy.

"This is Mr. Sniff.

He is a detective.

He is on a case.

He needs the keys

to all the rooms."

"Here they are," said Jill.

"Thank you," said Mr. Sniff.

Jill sneezed

and took a pill from her pocket.

She drank it down with some soda.

Mr. Sniff and Andy

went up the stairs

to the second floor.

18

They knocked on the door to Room 21.

"Excuse me. I am Mr. Sniff.

I am a detective.

I am working on a case.

May we come in?"

"Yes, of course,"

said the guest in Room 21.

"I am Sergeant O'Hound.

I am a policeman.

I am on vacation."

Mr. Sniff looked all over the room.

Then he looked at the bed.

"Hmm," he said.

"The top half is thicker

than the lower half."

He pulled back the blanket and sheet.

"There is only one sheet!

Someone has folded it over

so you can't get in!

22

Who makes the beds, Andy?"

"Jill does," said Andy.

Sergeant O'Hound sneezed.

"Sorry," he said.

"It is my hay fever."

Mr. Sniff looked at the flowers

on the table.

"Andy," he said,

"are there flowers in every room?"

"I think so," said Andy.

"Mother buys them at the farm market."

"Some of them, at least,"

said Mr. Sniff.

He gave Andy some flowers.

"Take these with you, please.

Thank you for your trouble, Sergeant.

Have a good vacation."

Mr. Sniff and Andy

went into many rooms.

If the guests were out,

Mr. Sniff opened the door

with one of Jill's keys.

He was careful

not to disturb anything.

At last they came to Room 13.

"This is our room," said Andy,

"and these are my brothers.

Wolf and Garson are twins.

28

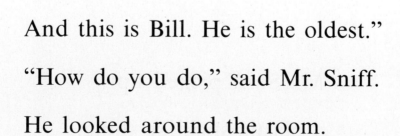

And this is Bill. He is the oldest."

"How do you do," said Mr. Sniff.

He looked around the room.

Mr. Sniff picked up

a plastic sticklike thing.

30

"Hmm," he said to himself.

"I wonder what this is for!"

Then he turned to Andy.

"Where do you sleep?" he asked.

"I sleep in the top bunk," said Andy.

"It is very hot.

I sometimes sleep outside

under a tree."

Mr. Sniff looked at his watch.

"It is late," he said.

"The tide is rising.

I am going for a swim."

"Can I come with you?"

asked Andy.

"Please do," said Mr. Sniff.

"I will meet you at the beach."

Mr. Sniff put down his umbrella,
his chair, and his towel.

"I am ready," said Mr. Sniff.

33

He and Andy ran into the water.

A swimmer with white curly hair

floated by on a tube.

"Afternoon," the swimmer said.

"Dr. Small is the name.

Staying up at Mutt's Motel, are you?"

"Yes," said Mr. Sniff.

35

"Have you seen the green, slimy thing?"

asked Dr. Small.

"Why—no," said Mr. Sniff.

"It comes by my window every night,"

said Dr. Small.

"Scares *some* people.

Green shiny face!

Hair like wet snakes!

But when I call,

it goes away and hides."

"Very interesting," said Mr. Sniff.

After his swim

Mr. Sniff went back to his umbrella

and put lotion on his nose.

"Let us take a walk, Andy," he said.

Andy and Mr. Sniff

walked along the beach.

They did not talk much.

Finally, Andy asked,

"Would you like some bubble gum?"

"No, thank you," said Mr. Sniff.

He was standing in the water,

looking down.

"What are these, Andy?"

asked Mr. Sniff.

"Mole crabs," Andy said.

"When the waves wash over them,

they put their antennas

up through the sand

to catch their food."

"Very clever," said Mr. Sniff.

He and Andy

took another swim.

Then Mr. Sniff went to the office

of Mutt's Motel.

"Hello, Hilda," he said to Mrs. Mutt.

"May I see your lipstick?"

"Here it is," said Mrs. Mutt.

Mr. Sniff tasted it.

"Very pretty color," he said.

Just then the door opened.

Some new guests came into the office.

The baby hit the call bell.

It did not ring.

Mr. Sniff turned the bell over

and felt inside.

"Of course," he said.

"The case is solved!

44

I will tell you how tonight.

Please ask all your guests

to come to the beach at nine o'clock.

And ask your boys to make a fire."

The moon was full.

Madame Bassett, Sergeant O'Hound,

Dr. Small, and all the other guests

were on the beach.

Jill came with her boyfriend.

Wolf and Garson,

Bill and Andy

made a huge fire.

45

"Where is Mr. Sniff?" asked Mr. Mutt.

"HERE!" cried a voice.

"That is it!" shouted Dr. Small.

A shiny green head

with hair like wet black snakes

was coming toward them.

It glowed in the dark.

"It is a wonder," said Mr. Sniff,

"what a plastic light stick

and some seaweed can do.

You snap it in the middle

and shake it up a little,

and it starts to light.

People use them on roads at night

when their cars stall,

or just for fun.

It had the letter A

written on it.

I found one in the boys' room."

Andy hung his head.

Mr. Sniff put his arm

around Andy's shoulder.

"Andy?" said Mrs. Mutt.

"Did *you* do all those things?"

"Yes," said Andy.

"But how did you find out,

Mr. Sniff?"

"First, I asked myself

who *could* have done it,"

said Mr. Sniff.

"Jill could have—

she makes the beds!

Sergeant O'Hound's bed was tricked.

Mrs. Mutt could have—

she wears Smooch!

The lipstick on Madame Bassett's

bathroom mirror was Smooch.

I tasted it myself.

In fact, *all* the Mutts

could have done it.

They all know

where the keys are.

Next I asked myself

who could *not*

have done these things.

I found yellow ragweed

mixed in with the flowers

in many rooms.

Someone who does not get hay fever

put it there.

Jill, you get hay fever.

I saw you take a pill.

So I did not think

it could be you."

"How did you know it was Andy?"

asked Mr. Mutt.

"It had to be someone,"

said Mr. Sniff,

"who does not get hay fever,

who knows where to find lipstick,

who is not afraid

of spider crabs or jellyfish,

and someone who likes to play

with light sticks.

Then I found bubble gum

inside the bell in the office.

Someone put it there

so it would not ring.

Only Andy chews bubble gum.

The case was solved."

"Why did Andy write 'Help! Help!'

on my mirror?" Madame Bassett asked.

"Because he wanted help!

Mutt's Motel is all filled up.

Andy has to sleep in the top bunk.

It is very hot there.

"Sometimes he sleeps

under a tree outside.

Room 13 is very small

for four growing boys."

"I am sorry," said Andy.

Mrs. Mutt hugged Andy.

"As soon as we can," said Mr. Mutt,

"we will give each of you boys

a room of your own."

"Wonderful!" said Madame Bassett.

"Families are important!"

said Sergeant O'Hound.

"Now," said Mr. Mutt,

"marshmallows for everyone."

Mr. Sniff said,

"Not for me, thank you.

I want to watch

the ghost crabs in the sand.

They only come out at night.

So I will say good night."

Andy followed Mr. Sniff.

He took him by the hand.

"Thank you, Mr. Sniff," he said.

"I am glad you are my friend."